Sarah S.  Baker

**The Boy Friend or All Can Help**

Sarah S. Baker

**The Boy Friend or All Can Help**

ISBN/EAN: 9783337058234

Printed in Europe, USA, Canada, Australia, Japan

Cover: Foto ©Andreas Hilbeck / pixelio.de

More available books at **www.hansebooks.com**

# THE BOY FRIEND;

## OR,

## ALL CAN HELP.

BY AUNT FRIENDLY,

AUTHOR OF "TIMID LUCY," "FIDGETTY SKEERT," &C.

---

"Know them which labour among you.   Esteem them very
highly in love, for their work's sake."

---

PHILADELPHIA:
WILLIAM S. & ALFRED MARTIEN,
606 CHESTNUT STREET.
1862.

# CONTENTS.

## CHAPTER VIII.

## CHAPTER IX.

## CHAPTER X.

## CHAPTER XI.

## CHAPTER XII.

## CHAPTER XIII.

## CHAPTER XIV.

## CHAPTER XV.

# THE BOY FRIEND.

## CHAPTER I.

### AN ICY MORNING.

ICE! ice! everywhere! Ice on the ground, ice on the trees, ice on the fences—the very houses coated with ice! So it was at Meedville, one Sunday morning in December, yet the church-bell rang out as cheerily as if it were the merry month of May, and the gate to the churchyard was thrown as wide open as if the broad walk were not one sheet of treacherous ice, promising a downfall to any who dared to venture upon it. A heavy mist was in the air, and there

2

was a continual rattling sound, as the trees dropped morsels of their frozen coating, when their branches waved in the wind.

Would anybody venture out on such a day? The sexton seemed to think so, for he pulled the bell-rope as if he was sure that he was accomplishing a good end.

At Meedville there were some church-goers who never staid at home for wind or weather, and Mrs. Berridge and her family were among them. The good lady herself, and her two daughters, would as soon have thought of putting out their own eyes, as neglecting the sound of that well-known bell. In their seats they were sure to be when the minister entered the chancel; that is, their bodies were sure to be there, wherever else their minds might chance to be wandering.

On this particular morning they had a stranger with them; not one of the tall, dignified men, or the fashionably dressed ladies, who occasionally appeared there, but a lad, in his grey roundabout—a boy, evidently not more than fourteen years of age.

The stranger seemed to think himself enough of a gentleman to walk up the middle aisle in advance of the party, and throw wide open the door of the third pew, for Mrs. Berridge and her daughters to pass in. This feat Miss Augusta Berridge accomplished without any injury to her garments in squeezing through the narrow passage. Little Annie followed, imitating her sister's movements with great care, and perching herself at length on the seat, with a satisfied air, as if the business of the morning was over, and now she had nothing to do but look about her, and see who was at church.

Annie had moved her head from side to side, and pointed with her nose at all the people down one aisle, and had actually counted twenty, when she noticed that her cousin Charlie was still on his knees. What could he be about all this time?

It did not once cross Annie's mind that Charles Clement was entering, for the first time, a church where he expected to worship for a whole year, and that he might feel this an occasion for special prayer. She could not know that he was asking that he might ever find his Heavenly

Father near him in that humble sanctuary, and that he might be himself a faithful hearer of the messages which the appointed clergyman should bring to his soul.

Of course Annie Berridge could not know all this; she did not even guess it, for to serious thoughts she was herself a stranger. Moreover, she had not in the least suspected that her cousin Charlie was of what she called "a religious turn." She had not seen him, so far as she could remember, till the evening before, and then he had been so merry and agreeable, that she fancied he must always be in a frolic.

Charlie Clement knew that there was "a time to laugh," and that this was not a suitable time he plainly thought; for when Augusta Berridge

2*

turned her face towards him, and gave it a comical, dolorous twist, as the minister entered the chancel, there was a very sober look in his eye, instead of the answering smile she expected.

The service went on. Charlie did not see Augusta passing her quick glances over the congregation; he did not notice the quiet munching of candy with which Annie contented herself; nor did he see that Mrs. Berridge's thoughts were far from the book on which her eyes were bent.

Mrs. Berridge had a respect for religion. She liked a devout manner in church. She wanted to set a good example; but she had not come up to the Lord's house to praise him for his mercies, and to call upon him

for forgiveness, and for that Holy
Spirit he delights to bestow on all
who ask it. Her service was vain,
fair as it was in outside show.

For once there was a true wor-
shipper in Mrs. Berridge's pew.
Augusta looked at her cousin Charles
in astonishment. He seemed really
interested in what he was about, and
when the sermon began, he listened
as if he wanted to hear; he listened
respectfully, like one who expected
to be taught a lesson worth learning.

The young clergyman was by no
means unattractive in appearance.
There was a look of earnest thought
about his face, but no traces of genial
warmth, or of any kind of consciousness of the outer world. During the
prayers he was forgotten, for he
spoke with quiet simplicity; but in

the pulpit he seemed declaiming, rather than addressing the people on a matter of moment to them. His sermon was a fine essay on the beauty of divine truth, but seemed intended to reach no particular class of persons, and to produce no particular effect.

"O, how good it is to get out into the fresh air!" exclaimed Augusta Berridge, as she stepped from the church door. "Dreadfully dull! Was it not, Charlie?"

Charlie was fairly startled by the sudden loud tones of his companion. A silence, that should have reproved, was his reply. He had been taught that there should be a reverent retiring from the house of God, as from the presence of a king; no noise in the ante-chamber, no rude haste in laying aside the garment of solemnity suited to such an audience.

"O! Cousin Charlie! Hold me up! I certainly shall fall!" said Annie, putting her foot timidly on the ice-covered steps.

The lad helped the little girl tenderly down, and then joined Mrs. Berridge and Augusta, who were waiting for him below.

"Isn't he tiresome—Mr. Mayer I mean," said Augusta, as they walked along.

"He cannot help it, my child. Poor young man! we must be patient with him. Nobody likes him, and I suppose he knows it. For my part, I am sorry for him, though it is quite a trial to have such dull preaching," said the mother.

Charles looked up in astonishment,

but said simply, "Has Mr. Mayer been long settled here?"

"Only half a year. The bishop recommended him, and the vestry took him without much thought. He stood high at the Seminary; why, I cannot imagine," was the reply.

"I should think he was a man of talents, and might be very agreeable in conversation," said Charles.

"Nobody knows much about that; he visits very little. He seems shy— uncommonly shy. I never could bear a bashful man," said Mrs. Berridge.

"I mean to go and see him," remarked Charlie; "I like to know my minister."

Augusta turned her sharp black eyes quickly upon Charlie, to see if he was smiling, but he looked perfectly sober, and she began to laugh, saying,

"I think I see him going through the torture of your visit. First he rises, as if he had a cramp in the knees; then out goes his arm, as if it were jerked out with an invisible string. Before you have time to fairly shake his hand, down it drops, and he looks you straight in the eyes, as if to ask you, what's your business. May I go with you?"

"No, no! But, cousin, I really mean to go," replied Charlie; and so the conversation ended, as the family had reached Mrs. Berridge's pleasant home.

## CHAPTER II.

### A BOYISH VISITOR.

CHARLES CLEMENT was the oldest son in a family of six, and his mother was a widow. It was not strange that he felt himself quite a man, as for three years he had been his mother's companion, and frequently her adviser. The younger children looked up to him as a remarkable person, and many of his schoolmates and friends were of the same opinion.

That Charlie was not at all diffident of his own powers, was plain from his decided step, and the particularly erect manner in which he carried his plump but well-formed figure. There was nothing of pride or arrogance, however, in his air, and in his round cheerful face there was a bright, sunny expression, which seemed to promise a willingness to think kindly of others as well as of himself.

Charlie would have packed up his trunk, if occasion had required, and travelled from Maine to Georgia alone, as composedly as if he were a person of forty. He had so long done the honours in his own home, and kept a watchful, protective eye upon his mother, that there was a kind of manliness about him uncommon in a lad of his age.

When he dressed himself on Monday morning, with particular care, before paying his intended visit to the rector, he had no idea that he

3

was about doing a thing from which any boy would shrink.

He had no difficulty in finding the humble lodging of Mr. Mayer: humble, for though the people of Meedville expected a minister un-equalled in talent and piety, they had no idea of giving him a salary which would be more than a bare subsistence.

Charlie knocked twice before any notice was taken of his arrival. It was plain that it was Monday in every sense of the word in that esta-blishment, a true washing-day, when all things must give way to the weekly purification. A little woman with a bonnet on, and a wet dress pinned up round her waist, at length made her appearance from the rear of the house. She opened her eyes

with astonishment, when instead of
the supposed "fish-man," Master
Charlie Clement stood before her,
with his cap in hand.

"Is the Rev. Mr. Mayer at home?"
said Charlie, with his usual com-
posure.

"Yes. I don't know. Yes, I'll
see," said the woman, in evident
confusion; whether at her own la-
mentably moist condition, or at the
unwonted appearance of a visitor at
that time, on a Monday morning, it
was hard to decide.

The woman of the bonnet disappeared at a side-door, without asking
the stranger to walk in. Master
Charlie, however, made bold to take
a few steps into the hall, and there
he awaited her return.

He had stood there just long

enough to note the thread-bare condition of the faded carpet, and the paintless arms of the wooden chair, when, not the woman, but quite another person appeared. A tall young man, in a calico dressing-gown, came out from the aforementioned side-door, and looked inquiringly at Charlie.

Charlie did not at first recognise in the person who stood before him, the Rev. Mr. Mayer of the preceding day. The young man was very pale, and a mass of dark hair was standing in wild confusion, straight off from his forehead, and his brown eyes stared absently, as if he had just been roused from sleep. The fact was, he had been deep in the composition of a sermon. His head had been resting on his hands, and his fingers thrust into his hair, when he was called to see "some young chap at the door, asking for the minister."

"Is this the Rev. Mr. Mayer?" said Charlie, after a moment of doubtful silence.

"Yes, yes," said Mr. Mayer, struggling to keep a most appropriate "thirdly" for the sermon out of his mind, and to attend to the matter in hand.

"My name is Charles Clement," said the lad, stepping forward, and putting out his hand.

A name all unknown to fame, it seemed to be to Mr. Mayer. He did not see the offered hand, but said,

"Well, sir, what is it, this morning?"

3*

"Perhaps I have come upon you at a busy time," said Charles, politely.

"I *was* writing, but"—and the minister looked inquiringly at the boy, "but I can attend to you now."

"I have no particular business, I can call at some other time," said Charlie, retiring.

Mr. Mayer gave a puzzled look at his visitor, and driving the "thirdly" fairly from his thoughts, said pleasantly,

"Wont you walk in now?"

"I thank you, not this morning, sir," said Charlie, decidedly, "but I should like to come again, for I want to know my minister."

As he spoke he again put out his hand, and looked up frankly into Mr. Mayer's face.

Mr. Mayer took the offered hand, and said, shyly,

"Yes, come again, I shall be glad to see you."

Another bow, and a pleasant "good morning" from Charles, and the interview was over.

Charlie Clement was more amused than annoyed at the result of his proposed call on the rector. He had made a beginning, and he was not disheartened.

# CHAPTER III.

## A STEP NEARER.

MRS. BERRIDGE had thought it necessary to introduce her nephew at the academy, where he was to be a pupil. Charlie would by no means have hesitated to appear there alone, but he politely assented, when his aunt proposed to accompany him.

Some domestic duties had kept her at home on Monday morning, and Charlie, as we have seen, took the opportunity to put in a wedge towards an acquaintance with his rector.

If Mr. Mayer had been spoken of respectfully, the lad would have felt inclined to treat him with all due

deference; indeed he had been taught
that a certain peculiar politeness and
reverence was due to those whose
office it is to minister in spiritual
things.

The light and unkind manner in
which Mr. Mayer had been mentioned, had, however, called out a
warmer feeling in Charlie Clement,
than might otherwise have been
aroused. He resolved, for his part,
to treat his minister with respect
and affection, and to be by no means
influenced by what others might say
about him.

As to the further prosecution of
his acquaintance he was somewhat
puzzled. Though by no means of a
bashful nature, he hesitated about
risking another call, where such visi-
tations seemed most unexpected, if

not unwelcome. Time for calling anywhere, Charlie had little or none that week, after he had fairly entered upon his studies. Although he did not "consume the midnight oil," it was after nine o'clock before his books were laid aside, and he was ready to fall into such sound sleep as only happy healthy youth can enjoy.

After this week of constant occupation, Saturday, with its holiday hours, was most welcome. Breakfast was hardly over, when Charlie produced a new pair of skates, and declared his intention of having enough good exercise to take the chill out of him for a week to come.

The boys on the neighbouring pond soon found out that the new scholar was likely to rank number one among the skaters, as well as in his classes. Such cutting of letters, such skilful manœuvres, had not often been seen on Meedville pond.

The academy bell at length called home the merry party to dinner. Tutor and pupils vanished like ice in a thaw. Charlie stopped to take a few more successful turns, after the coast was clear, and there was no danger of knocking over small boys and unskilful skaters, who did not know how to keep out of other people's way.

Dinner, however, was not a matter of entire indifference to Charlie Clement, and he too turned his face homeward. He had not gone far on his return, when he saw an old woman stepping cautiously along on the slippery path, at some distance before him. She had a basket on her arm, which, though evidently not heavy, made it more difficult for her to keep her balance. The wooden cane that she carried was but a poor security against a downfall on the treacherous ice which everywhere covered the ground. At length, after executing what seemed for the moment some extraordinary dancing steps, she fell, while basket and stick deserted her, and she lay helpless on the ground.

Charlie was at her side in a moment; but it was in vain that he tried to raise her.

"O my! I am done for! Dear! dear!" she exclaimed. "Now I never! What shall I do?"

"Do? why just get on my team here," said a cheerful voice at her side.

The speaker, a rough-looking countryman, was driving a wood-sled; and with a loud "whoa" to his horses, he jumped down, and began to suit his actions to the words. "Never fear, Katy Brown; you'll do well enough. You just got hoisted; that was all. Here now; so!" And his strong arms placed her on the sled, and leaned her against a meal-sack, which was now all the load.

"My, my! Jack—what's to become of my basket? What's *he* to do without his clothes, and Sunday coming. You could drive round by Meedville, I s'pose."

"How I wish I could, Katy," said the same hearty voice; "but you know I'm not my own master, and farmer Watkins don't let us idle our time."

4

"No more he don't, true enough!" said Katy, significantly. "I could lie by, to-morrow bein' Sunday; but what's to become of the clothes?"

"Where do they belong?" asked Charlie, giving a look at the great basket.

"They're his'n, the preacher's, of course. I don't wash for nobody else," said the woman.

"Mr. Mayer, do you mean?" asked Charlie, brightening.

"Yes, child; asking questions don't help, though," said the old woman, fretfully.

"But I mean to do more," said Charlie, taking up the basket; "I'll take them home for you."

"And I'll see to the old woman; so here goes;" and Jack Tyler raised his whip, as if to warn his horses to start.

Charlie turned towards Meedville with the great
basket on his arm. Page 31.

"Stop, stop! Where do you live?" said Charlie, addressing the woman.

"That aint no odds!" was the short answer.

"The first red house in among the pines, a piece along this road," said the man. "Shame, Katy, to speak so to the young gentleman.—She'll want looking after, likely enough," he added, in a whisper, not meant for Katy's ear.

"I aint too deaf to hear that," said the old woman, with a keen look; but it was plain that the words had escaped her.

Jack Tyler did not stay for any more conversation. He went his way; and Charlie turned towards Meedville, with the great basket on his arm.

Charlie Clement never troubled himself as to who laughed at him. All the boys in the village might have been hooting at him for carrying a washerwoman's basket, and he would not have cared. He was not naturally sensitive; and, moreover, when he was sure he was doing a kind action, the opinion of the world was of little consequence to him. He stood up, therefore, on the door-step of Mr. Mayer's boarding-house, on the main street, not noticing the crowd of boys who were coming down the sidewalk, full of holiday fun. A shower of snowballs first apprized him of their approach; and cries of "How much do you ask a dozen? Here goes the washer-boy!" &c., sounded in his ears.

"Six shillings a dozen! six shillings a dozen, my boys!" sang out Charlie, in a merry tone.

A face was seen for a moment at a lower window, and then the door was thrown open wide, and Mr. Mayer appeared.

The crowd of boys dispersed in a moment, and Charlie was about to give up his basket, when Mr. Mayer said, quite heartily, "Come in, come in." He had not forgotten the bright, pleasant face, that had looked so warmly at him the Monday before.

Charlie did step in; but it was only to explain how he became the bearer of the basket, and to say that he now had no time to spare, as his aunt's dinner hour had arrived.

"I want to go and see Katy," said

4*

Mr. Mayer, thoughtfully. "Do you know where she lives?"

"I could find it, I think. I mean to go there this afternoon," said Charlie, promptly.

"Then we will go together, if you like it," said Mr. Mayer.

"I should like it right well," said Charlie.

"At three o'clock, then, you will call for me," said Mr. Mayer.

"At three o'clock, sir. Good-bye, sir," was Charlie's reply.

## CHAPTER IV.

### KATY BROWN.

THREE o'clock found Charlie Clement punctually at Mr. Mayer's door, and the rector was there to meet him.

"I have often wanted to go to see Katy, but she never seemed to like the idea," said the rector, as they walked along.

"We may not get the pleasantest welcome in the world," said Charlie, smiling, "but the farmer's man seemed to think she might need help, for all that."

Charlie had often been with his mother to the homes of the poor, and to him the visit seemed quite a common occurrence. With Mr. Mayer, the case was different. During four years at boarding-school, he had prepared for four years at college; three more he had passed at a theological seminary. Motherless from his birth, he had never known the sweet joys of home, or the innocent pleasures of society. No loving hand had led him to the haunts of poverty, and taught him to minister to the poor.

Yet God had chosen Marshall Mayer to be peculiarly his servant, and the messenger of his mercy. The studious senior, at college, had become an earnest Christian; and when the world offered him a sphere where his talents might make for him a great name, he had chosen the ministry of Christ as his calling, and given up every object in life, save that of serving his heavenly Master.

While Mr. Mayer had been pronounced dry in the pulpit, and shy and unsociable in private life, his heart had been burning with a desire to do good. He had not been silent in his closet. Earnestly, faithfully, he had prayed to be made a fit instrument for the heavenly work, and to be guided in the path of usefulness. Such prayers are never unanswered. Marshall Mayer might seem for a time an unprofitable servant, yet he would not be driven out of the vineyard in shame and disgrace. He had to overcome the effects of a life of seclusion, and a natural sensitiveness, that was his constant scourge, ere he could be a useful pastor. Would he succeed?

Mr. Mayer found it a real pleasure to be walking through the clear cold air, with his cheerful companion at his side. With a lad like Charlie, his diffidence was not in his way, and conversation flowed naturally on. They had passed the village, and were on the country road, when Charlie asked,

"Is there to be a confirmation held here soon, sir?"

"The bishop is to visit us in February, but I do not know whether there will be any persons to be confirmed," said the rector, with a painful blush.

"I hope there will be one," said Charlie, and he took Mr. Mayer's hand as he spoke.

The boy's frank face was full of earnest feeling that was not to be mistaken.

"We must know each other better," said Mr. Mayer, with a hearty grasp of the hand that had been placed in his. "I hope that you may be that one, and be ready for the holy rite."

These few confidential words seemed to have placed Mr. Mayer and Charlie upon a different footing. The shy clergyman found himself talking freely to the boy at his side, of his hopes and his wishes, his purposes and his prayers.

Charlie felt the force of the deep piety that seemed to well up from his companion's heart, and his own resolution to devote himself to his

Master's service was strengthened and redoubled.

Katy Brown's red house among the pines was easily found, and there, at the window, sat Katy herself, knitting away, as if nothing had happened.

"We will go in, now we are here," said Mr. Mayer, who having screwed up his courage to the visit, was not willing to give it up.

Their knock was answered by a cry of "Come in," but no one appeared at the door.

The visitors obeyed, and found themselves in the single room, which was Katy's dwelling-place, her house truly; for it had a roof over it, and a chimney to carry up the smoke from her pipe and her fire.

The pipe Katy now laid aside, and

through her horn spectacles she looked up inquiringly at the visitors. The glance satisfied her as to who they were, and she hastened to say,

"Were not the clothes right, sir— Eh?" and she gave a doubtful look at Charlie.

"All right, Katy," said Mr. Mayer, helping himself to a seat, Charlie following his example. "All right; but I was afraid you were not right yourself, after your fall. Are you lame yet?"

"No more than I always am," said Katy quickly. "Old folks don't expect to be spry."

"And yet you take this long, cold walk every week. I had no idea you lived so far from the village" said Mr. Mayer, kindly.

5

"How should you know? You never were here before," said Katy.

"I thought you did not care to have visitors," said the minister, truthfully.

"No more I didn't," said Katy; "but now you are come, put up your feet to the fire afore you start away."

Mr. Mayer accepted the strangely offered courtesy, and drew his chair nearer to the wide chimney-corner.

"Are you not lonely here sometimes, Katy?" he said.

"Like enough, I am. Buryin' children aint a cheerful business, and I've done enough of it in my day. I shall be goin', too, soon," was the muttered reply.

"Going to a better country, I hope, Katy," said Mr. Mayer kindly.

"No such a thing! I aint one of the good ones," said the old woman. "I never was, and I'm too old now. I need n't expect nothin' better than I deserve."

The free, full forgiveness that Christ offers to sinners, was present to the young minister's mind. On that he built his own hope, and he longed to bring it home to the poor old creature before him, but she would not give him time.

"It aint no use!" she broke in upon him, as his lips parted. "It aint no use. I've worried and fretted all along of the years that is gone. If I was young I'd begin again. Take the right start, boy," she said, turning suddenly to Charlie. "Take a right start. Old folks can't learn new ways."

"I want to start right," said Charlie, earnestly.

The conversation was here interrupted by a loud double knock, followed by the immediate sound of Jack Tyler's heavy step on the floor.

Jack started back when he saw the visitors, but concluded, on the whole, to do his errand. With a side bow to Mr. Mayer, before speaking, he turned to Katy, and said, "It's like to be slippery as ever in the morning, Katy; I shall go to church in the old sleigh, and will take you along. Will you go? eh, Katy?"

"Like enough! like enough, Jack! But here, as you're in the way of of toting, maybe you'll give these folks a lift," and she looked significantly at her visitors.

It seemed that Katy was tired of

her company, yet she was half-pleased at their visit, too.

"If you can ride standin', sir, I'd be glad to have you on my sled," said Jack, with a bow to Mr. Mayer, that swept round far enough to include Charlie in the invitation.

"Thank you, thank you, we won't refuse such an offer," said Mr. Mayer. Then, going up to Katy, he shook her withered hand, and said, in a low, earnest voice, "Good-bye, Katy; remember it is never too late to begin a new life."

The old woman shook her head, but made no answer.

They saw her wrinkled face at the window, watching them as they mounted the sled, and Jack said, "She's glad to see you, for all she's so queer. The poor thing leads a

5*

lonesome life, and she likes to see
somebody now and then, if it's only
to say a cross word to."

Jack stood up firmly on his sled,
with the reins in one hand and the
whip in the other, but Mr. Mayer
and Charlie had to hold fast to the
upright poles at the corners of the
rude vehicle, to keep their footing.
Bump, bump, they went over the
rough masses of frozen snow, and for
a time conversation was quite impos-
sible. Mr. Mayer had food enough
for thought. He was dwelling on the
sight he had just witnessed—an aged
human being, ready to sink into the
grave, without hope, without one
cheering ray to lighten the dark
valley.

This painful subject so completely
occupied his mind, that he at first did

not even notice the conversation that arose between Charlie and the young countryman, as soon as they were on a smoother portion of the road.

Charlie was a lover of out-of-door sports, and was interested in all Jack could tell him of the fish in a trouting stream a mile or so away, or of the game that might be started in the very woods through which they were driving.

Then followed anecdotes of dogs, and Charlie grew quite animated in speaking of a former pet of his, who was so constantly with him that he had to be locked up on Sunday morning to keep him from following his master to Sunday-school.

"Sunday-school!" said Jack thoughtfully. "I always wished I'd a went when I was a boy."

We had a nice Bible-class at home, where there were two or three fellows as old as you," said Charlie.

Mr. Mayer had heard nothing while the talk was of game and dogs, but now a subject was touched upon more in unison with his own thoughts, and he became conscious of what was going on around him.

"A Bible-class, did you say, Charlie," and at the moment the thought struck the minister, that such an undertaking might be an instrument for good in his own parish.

"Yes, a Bible-class: our rector taught it; and how we all did enjoy it!"

Mr. Mayer was silent a moment. "I have no aptness in teaching. I never had a Sunday-school class. I am afraid it would be a failure," he thought. Still, conscience whispered, "You had better try. God can give strength for anything it is his will that we should do. Here seems to be an opening. Go forward."

"We might have a Bible-class here," said Mr. Mayer, thoughtfully.

"O, I should like it so much," said Charlie, heartily; "and you would go, wouldn't you?" he added, turning to Jack.

"I'd be a poor scholar enough," said Jack, giving a doubtful look at the minister.

"No one is a poor scholar who really wants to learn," said Mr. Mayer. "We will meet at my study to-morrow evening, and try to make a beginning."

"I'll be there, never fear," said Jack, decidedly.

At this moment they reached a side road, which turned off just as the scattered houses betokened the entrance to Meedville.

"I go this way," said Jack, turning his horses' heads towards the corner, and bringing them to a full stop.

"Then we must get off, and thank you for helping us so far on our way," said Mr. Mayer, stepping upon the crisp snow, as he spoke.

Away drove Jack, whistling as he went, while Mr. Mayer and Charlie walked on, side by side, talking of the Bible-class, until they reached the minister's door.

A bonnet had been thrust out of that same door every five minutes for the last half-hour, and a face within it had looked eagerly up the street.

The last look seemed to have been satisfactory, as it descried Mr. Mayer approaching, for the door was shut decidedly, and bonnet and wearer disappeared to the portion of the house where strangers were inadmissible.

"It is almost supper-time, I declare," said Mr. Mayer, looking wistfully at Charlie; "wont you stop and take a cup of tea with me?"

"Not to night, I thank you, sir. Aunt expects to have some company for me at home," said Charlie; and with an affectionate shake of the hand, he bade the rector good-bye.

Mr. Mayer's small study looked particularly attractive to him that evening. Perhaps it was because his good landlady, Mrs. Toombs, had taken the opportunity to give it a cleaning during his absence; perhaps it was because he was cheered by the knowledge that at last one of his parishioners was turning towards him with affectionate confidence. Even the tea-table seemed to him to have a more attractive air than usual, though Mrs. Toombs maintained her customary silence. Mrs. Toombs about her domestic duties, in her little brown hood, and stout apron, seemed quite another woman than Mrs. Toombs at the head of her table, in her clean white cap, and black alpacca dress; so entirely different a person that she did not seem to dare to open her lips, lest she should speak out of character. At any rate, something always kept her silent in the minister's presence. He might as well have taken his meals alone, for all the social element her society imparted; but she was useful in her way, and she knew it. She filled the rector's cup with tea before he perceived it was out, and kept his plate supplied with such fare as the table afforded, while he went on eating abstractedly, and lost in his own thoughts.

A slight rattling at the tea-tray was the general indication that supper was over, and he obeyed this hint as regularly as he did the bell that announced the meal in a state of readiness.

Mr. Mayer was very, very busy in his study that evening. Sermon after sermon he glanced at—none would suit him for the morrow. It was late before he saw what was before him; he must write, he must prepare a message that would reach at least one heart among his people; and after earnest prayer to Him who was to send that message, Mr. Mayer took his pen in hand.

The clock ticked not for him; not for him was the noise of the passer-by. He was lost, absorbed in the declaration of the good news to man-kind—a Saviour dying for the world, an ascended Lord calling all the weary unto him.

# CHAPTER V.

## POOR FUN.

AUGUSTA BERRIDGE was in the parlour, standing before the mirror. It was plain that she considered herself in full dress, in the sense of uncommonly well-dressed, and was altogether satisfied on that account. Augusta was wearing, for the first time, a skirt that swept the floor as she walked, and she had promenaded the room two or three times, looking over her shoulder to see the half a quarter of a yard of blue silk trail along the carpet. Annie, meanwhile, was equally occupied in endeavouring to catch glimpses of the great bow which tied her new sash.

They both started, and looked a little ashamed, as Charlie came in upon them, fresh from his long walk.

"Why, Charlie! you are not dressed!" said Augusta, in surprise.

"Am I late?" said Charlie, looking at his watch in a manly way, as if he had worn it always, (he had had it a month.) "Half-past five! I did not think it was so late. Moonlight and twilight coming together, misled me."

It did not take Charlie Clement long to make his toilet. With him it was a simple matter of business; to be well done, of course, but not to receive any unnecessary amount of thought. He was in the parlour before the first violent ring at the door announced that one of the guests had arrived.

The new-comer, Master Harry Dewitt, needed no one to introduce him.
It was plain that he and Augusta
were old acquaintances, and Charlie
he had already seen at school.

Harry Dewitt was very tall for
fourteen, and he did not seem
ashamed of his height, for he held up
his head, and was as straight as a
militia colonel on parade.

"Where were you this afternoon
that you did not go skating?" said
Harry, taking a comfortable chair,
and settling himself in it.

"I walked into the country with
Mr. Mayer," said Charlie frankly.

"With Mr. Mayer!" said Harry,
holding up both hands. "I don't
envy you the job."

"That's the kind of business that
suits Charlie," said Augusta, laugh-
6*

ing.  "He pretends to be very much pleased with Mr. Mayer."

"I do like him heartily," said Charlie, warmly.  "I wish I could see more of him."

Harry gave a low whistle, and Augusta shrugged her shoulders.

The boys and girls now came in by twos and threes, until all the guests had arrived.  Thirteen bright young faces were gathered round the table, all full of life and merriment.

Harry Dewitt was about to say what he considered a capital thing, when Augusta gave him a sudden nudge, and pointed significantly at Charlie.

Charlie was standing opposite to his aunt.  Mrs. Berridge waved her hand, and there was a moment of silence.

In a few simple words Charlie returned thanks for the blessings showered by the Divine hand, and then he took his seat as unembarrassed as if he had but spoken to some human being at his side. Charlie had so long been accustomed to saying grace at his mother's table, that it seemed to him a kind of matter of course, a pleasant part of the meal, not to be omitted. Mrs. Berridge had been enough at Mrs. Clement's to be aware of this fact, and now, at her own table, she was glad to see carried out what she considered a proper usage, an excellent form.

Charlie Clement had been but a single week at Meedville, yet he was beginning to have his influence there. The slightest thread casts a shadow, and even a young person is ever doing something for good or evil, by his example.

A bold, determined, upright spirit like Charlie's, always has its admirers and its imitators. The best scholar and the best skater in the academy must wield a power strong for good or evil.

This short, simple prayer, had been for Charlie a kind of public profession, telling plainly on which side he stood. Did he lose the respect of his companions by it? There were two or three who smiled during the whole performance, and one little girl, more silly than the rest, had trouble to suppress a senseless giggle; but the effect on most of the company was to make them feel that Charlie Clement was a person to be looked up to, a person who knew his duty, and dared to do it.

Augusta Berridge had a great store of games at her command, and was herself most skilful in playing them all. There was no lack of fun among the young people, and Charlie Clement's cheerful, natural laugh, was heard again and again.

At length a new game was proposed. One of the company was to go out, and return personating some character, whom the rest were to guess, from the representation.

Harry Dewitt had paraded the room

"With head erect, you fancy how,
        Arms locked behind,
    As if to balance the prone brow,
        Oppressive with its mind,"

until all had shouted "Napoleon!"

Charlie Clement, with a lantern in his hand, had peered into every face, and had been hailed as Diogenes seeking an honest man. Aristides, writing his own name on a shield, and Anne Boleyn offering her slender neck to the executioner, had all been personated and recognised.

It was now Augusta Berridge's turn to go out. She soon returned, wearing an old cloth cloak, that hid even the much-admired trailing dress. A tall beaver hat was on her head. She had but to walk across the room, in a slow, peculiar gait, when cries of " Mr. Mayer! Mr. Mayer!" were heard from all sides of the room; but with this she was not content, but began, in a voice the exact counterpart of Mr. Mayer's, to say, "Dearly beloved brethren—"

"Now that is too bad, Augusta!" said Charlie, indignantly. "Mr. Mayer is our minister, and you owe him respect on that account, if you do not like him."

Augusta threw down the cloak and hat, and exclaimed, "I don't see why I may not have a little fun at his expense, if he is a minister!"

The king of a country revenges the disrespect offered to his herald, and a minister is the herald of the King of kings, and should be treated accordingly. I use my mother's words," said Charlie warmly. "I think you owe some respect to the office, Augusta, whatever you may think of the man!"

"What is all this?" said Mrs. Berridge, coming in at the moment.

"Only Charlie giving us a sermon," said Augusta, laughing.

"Go on, Charlie; I should like to be a hearer," said Mrs. Berridge, taking a seat on the sofa.

"No! No! let us play clements!" said Annie, who was impatient to have the frolic recommenced. A sight of an approaching tray called off her attention, and pyramids of ice-cream were soon the objects of general interest.

The company now broke up into little circles, and Charlie had an opportunity to carry out a plan which he had in his mind all the evening.

"Augusta was too hard on Mr. Mayer," said Harry Dewitt.

"Indeed she was," said Joseph White, the oldest boy in the company.

The conversation having turned upon the clergyman, after speaking affectionately of him, Charlie mentioned the Bible-class, and actually obtained a promise from Harry and Joseph, at least to try it for the first evening. Not that Harry and Joseph had the slightest desire to improve in the best of knowledge. Their Sunday evenings were dull at home; this would be an excuse for going out, and "might not, after all, be so bad," as they said to each other on their way home.

The Bible-class; that was the last thing in Charlie Clement's mind that night: not the frolic of the

7

evening, not angry feelings towards Augusta; but the Bible-class, a new opportunity of improvement, a new Sunday joy, a new step on the heavenly road.

## CHAPTER VI.

### GOOD SEED.

THE Sunday morning service was over, and the people of Meedville were scattering away to their homes. Mr. Mayer had preached on the encouraging words of our Saviour, "Whosoever cometh unto me, I will in no wise cast out." Simply, tenderly, earnestly, this blessed promise had been urged upon the attention of the hearers. The old, burdened with many years of sin, and the child just beginning to struggle with its evil heart, were called upon to accept the merciful invitation of Jesus, and trust themselves to him.

Annie Berridge had soon found

out that cousin Charlie was fond of children, and was never better pleased than when he had her at his side, or on his knee. That morning, he had passed a pleasant hour with her, telling her Bible-stories, and when she left him, full of thanks for his kindness, he had won from her a promise to "be a good girl at church, and try to listen to the sermon."

Annie had kept her promise, and Mr. Mayer's faithful words had for the first time stirred in her heart a yearning to be one of the Saviour's little ones, a wish to know something more of the meek and lowly Jesus. Augusta had not thought of listening either to service or sermon. Though bodily present during the time of solemn worship, her mind was far away, dwelling on the plans and pleasures of the week to come.

A habit of inattention at church! A trifling sin, as some would try to think it. Is it a trifling sin to insult the Most High in his own sanctuary? Is it a matter of no consequence to shut the ears to the voice of prayer, and turn the thoughts from the words of exhortation that might win the heart to better things? One great avenue of good, one great chance of improvement is taken away, when listless inattention becomes a habit in church.

Augusta was in her usual frivolous state when she left the church door, and out of the abundance of her heart her mouth spoke.

Annie paid but little attention, while her remarks were on the dress

7*

of acquaintances in the neighbouring pews, but when she began to speak of Mr. Mayer, her attention was gained.

" I do wish Mr. Mayer would go away, and somebody more interesting would come. My bones fairly ached before the sermon was over. I don't believe he knows what he is talking about himself."

Thoughtless words, Augusta would have called them, wicked words they were. Augusta would not have willingly pained her little sister's body, even by the scratch of a pin, yet she was now doing her soul a fearful wrong. Annie looked up to Augusta as much smarter and wiser than herself, and she felt ashamed that she had been moved by what Augusta seemed to think so tiresome. Her half-formed resolutions to be better were checked, the tender feeling at her heart passed away, and she was ready to add her idle words to those her sister was uttering.

Those gossipping talks at the church door, those needless criticisms on the sermon, their evil work will not be fully known until the judgment-day. If you cannot leave God's house yourself in a sober frame of mind, have pity on your neighbours, and do not drive away their good thoughts by your foolish conversation. If you have found the sermon dull and tiresome, keep back your complaints of weariness; the message which has not reached you may have touched a tender chord in the heart of your companion. Your disrespectful remarks on your minister may render his labours useless just when they were taking effect. " But when they have heard, Satan cometh immediately, and taketh away the word that was sown in their hearts."

This "snatching away" of the good seed at the church door and by the way-side, is truly Satan's work. Who would wish to work for and with the Evil One?

This was not Augusta Berridge's desire or intention, but what mischief may they not do, who never utter the prayers, "Cleanse thou me from secret faults," " Set a watch, O Lord, before the door of my lips!"

There was no more true worship for little Annie that day, and when she bade Charlie good-night, he saw that the tender, better look, that had stolen over at church, in the morning, was utterly gone.

Charlie had had a busy day. His Bible had been almost constantly in his hand. He had his usual reading in a course pointed out for him by mother, and then there was the Bible-class lesson, he wanted to be prepared on that.

Mr. Mayer had declared it his intention to make the "Christ of the Old Testament" the subject of his lessons, and Charlie had been puzzling over the books of Moses to find some traces of the promised Saviour. For prophecies he was looking, and he was quite discouraged at meeting so few of them.

Charlie was very familiar with the Scriptures, and he had perhaps fancied that he should astonish Mr.

Mayer by his knowledge. Charlie Clement had his own faults, just those that naturally rose from his energetic, self-confident nature.

Mr. Mayer sat in his little study, with two candles on the table before him. Mrs. Toombs had made up her mind that some new plan was on foot, and when Charlie Clement rang the bell at seven o'clock, she would by no means permit her "hired girl" to go to the door. Indeed, the duty of answering the bell, Mrs. Toombs generally preferred to perform herself. She felt herself mistress in her own castle, and so bound to look well to the out-posts.

Four times the bell had rung, and the four lads had appeared, and then Mrs. Toombs was left to quiet and curiosity for the rest of the evening.

Mr. Mayer had spoken in the pulpit till he was quite accustomed to it, but there was something that roused all his diffidence at the idea of having young faces so near to him. This feeling vanished, however, when Charlie Clement came in, with his frank, pleasant manner, counting on the three members of the Bible-class as so many treasures, in which he was part owner.

Mr. Mayer had never felt more solemn in his life, than when he knelt down with the four boys to ask the blessing of God on his new undertaking. When he closed with the Lord's prayer, Charlie Clement joined him, and the minister's heart thrilled with pleasure, as Jack Tyler's deeper tones were heard in the well-known petition. It is hard to talk of one's mother and one's home to uninterested hearers, much harder it is to speak of Christ and heaven to unresponsive listeners. It was cheering to Mr. Mayer to hope that at least half of his little class were ready to hear what he had to say.

At the Garden of Eden the lesson began. Mr. Mayer made the boys mark all the description of its beauty that is given, and then turn to the description of that second garden of bliss, promised in the Revelation to the followers of Jesus.

How were Adam and Eve, when driven from Paradise, to hope to walk by the river of the Water of Life, and eat of the fruit of that tree whose leaves are for the healing of the nations?

The promise given to our first

parents sprang to Charlie's lips, and Mr. Mayer's smile told him he was right:

"The seed of the woman should bruise the serpent's head. The Son of Man should triumph over the devil."

That Christ, suffering for sinners, might have been made known to Adam, Charlie had never thought; and when Mr. Mayer dwelt upon Abel's offering of a lamb, and Adam and Eve knowing their son's sacrifice to be a sign of the coming Redeemer, Charlie's eye brightened, and he exclaimed,

"O how beautiful! I like to think of that. I have always been so sorry for Adam!"

"We all try an experiment somewhat like the one through which

8

Adam passed. That is, we find out for ourselves that we cannot stand temptation. No one is ready to give himself up wholly to Christ, to be redeemed and sanctified, till he feels, like Adam, that he deserves to be driven from Paradise, and shut out by the angel with the flaming sword," said Mr. Mayer.

Jack's eyes were fixed on the speaker, but Charlie's were cast down. Had he ever fully realized that he was utterly unworthy of salvation? The question was not to leave him at once, it was to abide in his heart, demanding a fair and full answer.

Mr. Mayer had resolved that the Bible-class should have but a short meeting. The hour he had fixed upon had passed, yet no one looked pleased when the rector's Bible was closed, and the lesson was over. Even Harry and Joseph had been intellectually interested; but Jack and Charlie had felt their souls moved and enlightened. So sweetly rose the hymn that closed the exercises, that Mrs. Toombs stole into the hall to catch its sounds, and the passers-by owned it as most welcome on a Sabbath evening.

# CHAPTER VII.

## HOMELESS.

THREE weeks had passed pleasantly away for Mr. Mayer. He was getting better acquainted with his people. At Katy Brown's cottage he was a frequent visitor; with Jack Tyler he had many pleasant talks by the way, to which the Saviour, approving, listened. Charlie Clement was giving his minister the sunshine of his warm affection, and more than one friendly hand was reached out to the rector in his daily walks.

Saturday night had come, and full of thankfulness Mr. Mayer had gone to rest. His sleep was not to be uninterrupted. At midnight he was

roused by the cry of fire, and by the
sudden flashing of red light upon his
window. Yes, fire in all its terrors
was near him. Hastily dressing himself, he ran to the scene of desolation
and distress. Mrs. Toombs' house
was one of a row of low wooden
buildings that were crowded together
along the main street of Meedville.
The most remote of these dwelling-
houses was now in flames. The cry
that roused the rector had fallen on
the ears of many of his people, and a
crowd had already gathered, a helpless crowd, without an engine or an
adequate supply of buckets.

Some effort was made to subdue
the flames, but the pressing immediate necessity seemed to be to save the
inhabitants from a miserable death,
and to secure some of their property

8*

before it was too late. Mr. Mayer was foremost among those who plunged, amidst fire and smoke and falling timbers, to seek out children and aged sleepers, and to save the little all of the sufferers.

So rapidly the fire moved on, that Mrs. Toombs' house was in danger before the fire had consumed the building where it originated. Confused and terrified, the poor woman could do nothing but hold fast to her silver spoons and cry out for help. Mr. Mayer calmly lent his aid, and saw a portion of her furniture removed, before it was too late. The roof fell in at last with a crash.

Mr. Mayer had few earthly treasures, yet his books were precious to him. In his eagerness to save those who were in danger, and to help the distressed widow, with whom he had made his home, he had forgotten them.

Now a cheerful voice at his side exclaimed, "Your books are safe, Mr. Mayer. I looked after them as soon as I saw how the fire was spreading. They are all at our house."

Charlie Clement enjoyed that moment, and the "Thank you! thank you, Charlie!" that followed.

There was no lack of homes for the houseless that night. Beds of straw were exchanged for beds of down, and the rich made the poor welcome. Mrs. Toombs, however, preferred to walk a mile into the country, to "stay with one of her well-wishers," she said, rather than to accept Mrs. Berridge's invitation to follow the minister to her house.

Sunday morning came: the bell announced the hour of the accustomed service. This was surely no day on which to omit the voice of prayer and thanksgiving. Yet Mr. Mayer was weak and weary; his store of sermons had perished in the flames.

"What will Mr. Mayer do? he will break down certainly," said Augusta Berridge to her mother, as she took her seat in the pew.

Mrs. Berridge bowed her head, and managed to say, "We shall see," without any of the stir of a whispered conversation.

Never had Mr. Mayer so wholly lost himself in the service. The prayers he had so often spoken, came from his lips like the free breathings of his own devotional feelings. Self was forgotten in the duty of the present moment.

The time for the sermon came. While others had been sleeping away the fatigue and excitement of the fire, Mr. Mayer had been deep in meditation and earnest in prayer. He could have stood up that day before assembled nations, and opened his mouth, confident that it would be given unto him what to say in honour of his Divine Master.

Augusta Berridge cast her eye round the congregation as Mr. Mayer entered the pulpit. Many who had been wont to return her significant glances, were now looking towards the clergyman, as if they were expecting to receive a message which it was all-important for them to hear. Charlie Clement's eyes were cast down; he was silently praying that the Spirit of God might so guide and direct the speaker, that his words should be "words spoken in season," to bring much joy to many hearts.

Ah, if the critical hearers would cease to be on the watch for defects, and pray for him who is about to address them, then, indeed, might the preached word of God become a mighty engine for good.

Calmly Mr. Mayer gave out his text—"The Son of Man had not where to lay his head." The beggared and houseless were gathered in the church that day, with those who had tenderly felt for neighbours, thrust from their homes, and families suddenly left destitute.

The Saviour, a pilgrim without a refuge, was brought before them, and every eye was fixed, every ear was ready to listen.

Jesus, the King of heaven, seemed once more among them, sympathizing with the distressed, and cheering his true children to acts of kindness. Jesus, the ascended Lord, was calling on the homeless of earth to share his home in the skies, to ensure a place in the heavenly mansions, where sorrow cannot come.

Never had divine truth been so preached from that pulpit; never had those hearers so welcomed the good seed in honest hearts. There was no gossip at the church door that day. Satan snatched away no good seed by idle chat by the wayside.

# CHAPTER VIII.

## A FALL.

CHRISTMAS had showered its gifts in the lap of childhood, and breathed its whispers of sacred comfort to the more way-worn pilgrims of earth. The New Year had opened with its halo of hope, and its rainbow of good resolutions.

Two months had passed since Charlie Clement left his home on a Southern plantation, and came to the North to carry on the education that had been so thoroughly and wisely commenced.

His mother's kind, judicious influence no longer surrounded him like a protecting mantle. The freedom

9

from the faults of most boys of his age, which he had fancied to be the result of his own better balanced character, or the natural offspring of his principles, was to be sorely tested. The manliness which had been most attractive when it had developed in a son, guarding and sustaining a widowed mother, became less agreeable in the boy, left his own master, and ungoverned even by a soft maternal hand.

The idea of his own power and strength to do all, and know all, daily increased in Charlie. Augusta made sport of him, and called him "Mr. Pomperosity," and Annie looked up to him as the wonder he seemed to think himself; but Mr. Mayer saw with deep pain the change that was coming over his dear young companion. His gentle warning seemed to have no effect, yet he did not despair. His quiet influence might yet do something, and that he brought to bear, by being much in the society of the youthful parishioner, who was so dear to him. Mr. Mayer really believed that Charlie was a true child of God, and would not be suffered to fall a prey to the temptations of one great fault. For him he prayed most fervently, yet trembled while he prayed, lest only the severest discipline should bring back the wanderer to the humility of a follower of Jesus.

The time for the confirmation was approaching, yet Charlie was not very regular at the services the rector had appointed as a preparation for that rite; he seemed to think his preparation so thorough, that he needed no added word of counsel, no closer self-examination.

A bright Saturday, early in February, had come. The snow made white the country far and wide, and the merry sleigh-bells sounded out through the streets of Meedville, and over the glittering meadows.

Light "cutters" and fast horses were in requisition that day, and Charlie Clement had determined to have a ride. Early in the morning he engaged an establishment to his taste, and at two o'clock he appeared at Mrs. Berridge's door, as full of merriment as if life was all careless boyhood.

Augusta soon came out, all wrapped in furs, and full of smiles. Charlie was just handing her into the sleigh, in his best style, when Mrs. Berridge's face appeared at the parlour window. The sash was thrown up in a moment, and the mother exclaimed,

"Charlie, Charlie! stop! You are not going to drive Black Fury?"

"Why not? I am used to horses. Never fear, aunt, I know what I am about."

"But Augusta! I don't dare to trust you," began Mrs. Berridge. Charlie was by this time in his seat, and in another moment the spirited horse was moving down the street at full speed.

Mrs. Berridge cast a long, anxious glance after the little party, and did not move from the window until the sound of the bells died upon the ear.

The keen air and the rapid motion

9*

were exhilarating, and Charlie urged
on his horse at headlong speed.  He
had entered one of the lanes near
Meedville, when bells were heard
ringing loudly behind them.

Augusta turned her head, and exclaimed,

"It is Harry Dewitt!  Don't let
him pass us!"

There was no danger of any one's
passing Black Fury when he was
excited by the sound of horses' feet
behind him.  On he sped, as if unconscious of the light vehicle attach-
ed to him, while Charlie vainly en-
deavoured to rein him in.

· They were now beyond the beaten
road, and Charlie knew not which
way to steer among the snowdrifts
and gulleys which extended from
fence to fence.

Black Fury plunged madly on, the sleigh was but a plaything to the strong horse in his excitement. He stopped not even when it was turned on one side, and Augusta found herself lodged in a bed of snow. It would have been happy for Charlie if he had found as soft a resting-place. His arm caught in the reins as the sleigh went over, and with it he was dragged along, now dashed against the runners, now whirling through the snow, furrowing it as he passed. The reins broke at last, and Charlie was left senseless by the road-side.

Harry Dewitt had taken Augusta into his sleigh with some pride; he was not unwilling to have a little triumph over Charlie, who was particularly proud of his skill as a "whip."

Harry had no idea of following the mad course of Black Fury. "I ought not to risk Miss Augusta's life," he said to himself; but not without a feeling of shame, he turned his horse's head towards Meedville.

Charlie was not to lack a friend in his extremity. Jack Tyler had been out with his wood-sled, and had just turned a corner which led to the lane, when the maddened · horse, which Charlie had driven, dashed past him. Jack did not stop to pursue the horse, for he felt sure that he was needed in the contrary direction. On he went, plodding as fast as he could through the deep snow, leaving his trusty horses to follow him at their own gait.

Charlie did not know whose strong arms were folded tenderly around him. He did not see the honest face that was wet with tears as it bent over him. He could not know that eager observers appeared at the windows, as he was carried through Meedville, as helpless a burden as the wood upon which he was laid. Very different were his feelings when upon that humble sled, from those at his departure, so full of pride and joy.

Charlie Clement was restored to consciousness, to find himself the tenant of a body racked with pain, and stiffened in every limb. He knew his aunt was not fond of nursing; he knew it cost her stout figure an exertion to be moving continually; yet he had to see her waiting upon him, and to know that it was his own folly that had made him helpless as an infant. Even the keeper of the livery-stable had warned him against the horse he had chosen to drive, yet he had been willing presumptuously to risk his own life, and that of another. But he had been spared. O that thought! Charlie dwelt on it with deep gratitude, but gratitude mingled with bitter repentance. In the silence of his sick room a phantom seemed to rise before him, a phantom from which he would gladly have turned his eyes. He saw himself, full of presumption and self-importance, and he was sick at heart. Where was the modesty that is becoming in youth? Where was the humility, without which piety must become an empty name?

Charlie Clement saw himself, and he was humbled in dust and ashes;

but, blessed be God, when our eyes
are opened to behold our own sinful-
ness, He pours into them the light of
the Sun of Righteousness, and com-
forts with this vision of mercy and
redeeming love.

Now came the faithful words of
a friend. Mr. Mayer did not say,
"Peace! peace!" until he was sure
that the arrow of heaven had pierced
even to the depths of the soul. He
brought home the rebuke that was
needed, before he poured in the oil
of consolation.

Charlie Clement had learned this
lesson;—No religious habits, no
faithful training, can keep the young
Christian from sin. He falls when
exposed to temptation, unless watching unto prayer, and upheld by the
power that sitteth in the heavens.

Charlie's fall might seem little to lookers on, but he knew himself how far he had wandered from the true spirit of a follower of Christ. Humble as a little child he lay in his sick room, while others were to enjoy the privilege of openly professing themselves servants of the "meek and lowly Jesus."

# CHAPTER IX.

## THE CONFIRMATION.

THE church at Meedville was crowded. Many had come merely as spectators to the confirmation service; many more as devout worshippers. The bishop stood in the chancel. The persons to be confirmed were called on to come forward. A sunburnt youth, whose broad shoulders proved him familiar with toil, walked slowly up the aisle. No faltering thought, no fear of man, slackened his usual bold, firm tread. He moved gently, to keep pace with the aged woman who leaned on his arm.

Poor, and coarsely clad, was Katy

10

Brown. There was no charm in her dark and wrinkled features, yet at her Mr. Mayer looked tenderly and anxiously, as she drew near the chancel. In that worn and weary body was an immortal soul, a soul that had been brought into the fulness of the gospel light. Yes, that aged woman was the first fruits of Marshall Mayer's ministry, and he rejoiced over her with great joy. Jack, he had guided and directed, but to Katy, it had been his blessed privilege to declare the truth, as it is in Jesus.

Who can describe the devout interest of the faithful pastor as he heard the words, "Defend, O Lord, this thy servant, with thy heavenly grace, that she may continue thine for ever, and daily increase in thy

Holy Spirit more and more, until she come unto thine everlasting kingdom."

For Jack there might yet be a hard struggle, a battle "unto blood" with temptation; but the old pilgrim was near her journey's end. She had but the dark valley to pass, and she would enter into the reward purchased for the penitent by the blood of Jesus.

O, the riches of the mercy of Christ! Who would not enlist under this Captain of our salvation? Who would not labour in the vineyard of such a Lord?

# CHAPTER X.

## ANNIE'S WORK.

"It is almost worth while to have been shut up so long, to be so glad to be with you all again," said Charlie Clement, with one of his old bright smiles.

The family circle upon which Charlie looked was indeed a cheerful one. Gathered about the centre-table sat Mrs. Berridge, Augusta, and Annie, each as busy as if convinced that industry was the secret of happiness. Mrs. Berridge was knitting an Afghan, and the portion of her completed work lay across her lap, its gay stripes seeming the brighter for the brilliant gas-light

that fell upon them. Mrs. Berridge
was just one of those ladies who
seemed most in her place when sitting in her own parlour, occupied
about some pretty work. There was
a quiet, settled look in her stout
figure, and a sort of .repose in her
face, that made one feel rested to look
at her.

Augusta, on the contrary, was all
animation; when her mouth opened,
her black eyes sparkled, and her slender note seemed to grow sharper, and
do its part towards the vivacious expression of her face. Augusta was
drawing, and she handled her pencil
with a skill that made it a pleasure
to watch her.

Charlie took up the spirited head
of Apollo, which she was just finish-
ing, and gave it the glance of a con-

10*

noisseur. He was about to hazard some criticisms, and to make some mythological allusions, that were more calculated to show his own powers, than to please the hearers, when there was a whisper at his heart that checked him. With a well-deserved ˙compliment on the execution, he handed it back to Augusta, who took it with a laugh, and said,

"I think Mr. Pomperosity died in your sick room. Do you think that one of the Siamese twins will be able to live without the other. Eh, Charlie?"

"I hope so," said Charlie, soberly.

"You ought not to call Charlie names," said Annie, looking protectively at her cousin.

"You need not stand to your arms

on all occasions, Annie, when Charlie is spoken to," said Augusta, not very pleasantly.

"Annie and I are fast friends," said Charlie, with a fond look at his little cousin. "Come, Annie, let me see your work?"

Annie thrust her hands under the table. Her work was not truly such as would please an artist's eye. She was embroidering on a piece of brown broadcloth such flowers as no botanist could have recognised; even the leaves were of angular forms, which might be sought for in vain in nature.

Annie was a fat, comfortable, tender-hearted little girl of ten, but by no means sensitive. Charlie could not account for the sudden bashfulness that had overtaken her.

At Charlie's urgent request she exhibited her work, and reluctantly owned that she was making a watch-case.

"A watch-case!" said Augusta, with a laugh, "I thought it was a bag for some baby's silver porringer, or, perhaps, a sacred retreat for some worthy potato, to which a small specimen of the same kind had grown fast. Who is it for, pray?"

"Let me see if it will fit," said Charlie, taking out his watch, and slipping it into the case.

"The watch is like truth, hid in a well," said Augusta. "It can't be for you, Charlie, so draw your watch up from the depths."

"Don't say any more about it, Charlie," whispered Annie, beseechingly.

"Who will go and get my books for me?" said Charlie. "I am in a studying mood."

Annie hastened to oblige her cousin, while Augusta laughingly said,

"I wonder Mrs. Toombs allows Mr. Mayer to come here to hear you recite. I don't think she has ever forgiven us for keeping him that whole fortnight after the fire. She is a queer being. I wonder what such people were made for?"

"Made to do some particular good work, no doubt," said Charlie. "But here comes my books, and I must go to studying in earnest."

Charlie had never studied so faithfully as since Mr. Mayer had kindly offered to act as his tutor until he should be able to reappear at the academy. Charlie's perfect recitations left time enough during the appointed hour for much that was interesting in the way of explanations. Often the hour closed with a pleasant, profitable talk between the minister and his young parishioner, which was to have its impression when the things of this world have passed away.

# CHAPTER XI.

## ANNIE'S VISIT.

THE fire which had burned Mr. Mayer's sermons, and left him without a home, had been by no means an enemy. The sermons that he had laboured over at the seminary, or wrought out in his study since his arrival at Meedville, had been profitable to his mind, by way of discipline, but with them his heart had had little to do. They were fit for the fire; like a boy's old latin exercises, they had fulfilled their end, and were to be cast aside for better things.

Mr. Mayer now knew his people. He loved them, he felt for their wants, and to them he spoke, when he entered the pulpit, for them he wrote in his study. They knew that they were directly addressed by a friend who had their best interest at heart, and they listened, and took home his earnest appeals and faithful counsel.

Members of the parish who had thought little of their minister or his home, had their sympathies called out towards him, when his wardrobe was burnt, his study furniture destroyed, and he was forced to accept the kind invitation of Mrs. Berridge to make her house his home.

Mrs. Toombs soon found a house placed at her disposal, at an uncommonly low rent, and found other hands than hers interested in providing for the rector's comfort.

No one acknowledged who had placed the new suits in his bedroom closet. No one claimed the credit of new furnishing the study. Stout farmers and country shopkeepers who had given themselves no concern about their minister when he seemed comfortable, had found pleasure in relieving him in his unexpected difficulties. They knew what they had done, and they felt an added interest in one for whom they were able to do something.

And Mrs. Berridge, had she no part in this work of love? Apparantly none; yet Mr. Mayer received through the post-office a blank envelope containing a fifty dollar

11

note; from whom else could it have come?

These nameless kindnesses made Mr. Mayer feel that he was among friends, and his stiffness gave way to a frank and kindly manner that strengthened the pleasant relations growing up between him and his people.

Mr. Mayer was sitting in his study one morning in April. There was a timid ring at the door. Mrs. Toombs was at her post in a moment; motioning back the "hired girl," who was peeping after her, round the corner of the entry, the little woman opened the door. There stood Annie Berridge, looking by no means as calm and comfortable as usual.

"Is Mr. Mayer at home?" asked the little girl.

"Yes. What shall I tell him?" said Mrs. Toombs, standing in front of Annie.

Annie fumbled nervously at a little parcel in her hand, and then repeated her question,

" Is Mr. Mayer at home?"

Mrs. Toombs was suspicious of any intercourse between her lodger and Mrs. Berridge's family. She seemed to have conceived a vague notion that there was a plan to decoy him away, which it was her duty to check in the bud. She now looked at the parcel most significantly, and said,

"Shall I give it to him?"

Annie was about to render up,

helplessly, her treasure, when Mr. Mayer himself appeared.

It would have been a great disappointment to Annie to go away without an interview, and her face grew proportionably bright at the sight of the rector's face.

"Come in, Annie, how do you do this morning?" he said, kindly taking her hand. The air was chilly, and there was a cheerful wood fire on the study-hearth. "Come and warm your fingers," said Mr. Mayer, drawing Annie towards the bright flame.

Mrs. Toombs fidgetted uneasily, but retreated down the hall, at length, without even speaking to the "hired girl," who was still at her post of observation.

It seemed to take Annie a great while to warm her hands. She held

"I made this for your watch."  Page 117.

them up before the fire long after
they were perfectly comfortable. The
package had been hastily thrust into
her pocket. She had given a most
minute and satisfactory account of
the health of all the family, before
she could make up her mind to begin
the ceremony of presentation. As to
this same ceremony, she had given
herself much thought, and had plan-
ned exactly what she would say;
now, however, her most suitable remarks had forsaken her, and she
could only stammer out,

"I made this for your watch, and
so I came to bring it."

Mr. Mayer unfolded the little parcel, and took out the result of Annie's labours. Such a watch-case had
not often been seen, yet Mr. Mayer
looked at it with as much pleasure as

11*

if it were an exquisite work of art. He knew that love had prompted the gift, and it was very precious.

Affection was all the more welcome to Mr. Mayer, because he had been so long alone in the world, a mere student, without a family circle or a home. Affection he prized for its own sake; he moreover knew that if he wished to lead his young parishioners heavenward, they must place their hands lovingly and trustfully in his.

Now, he looked very kindly at Annie, as he thanked her for her gift.

"See, how nicely it fits," he said, as he placed his great silver watch in the case. "You could not have done better if you had taken its measure."

Annie looked curiously at the watch, and Mr. Mayer put it in her hand. The watch was covered with deep chasings, and was as thick as two watches, such as are now made.

"This was my grandfather's watch," said Mr. Mayer, opening it, and showing the works. Annie watched the silent motion of the wheels, while Mr. Mayer went on to say,

"So it went, tick, tick, when my good grandfather was alive. His wonderful body wore out, and was laid in the grave, yet here the watch is going, going still. Does a watch then last longer than a man?"

Annie looked up suddenly, as she answered,

"Yes! No! A kind of a way."

"It lasts longer than a man's body, but the watch has no soul to live for ever, when it is worn out," said Mr. Mayer. "It is only made for use in this world. Yet how carefully we use it, what pains we take lest it should be injured. Is not a soul worth as much trouble? It needs to be guarded and kept from harm, too; but does it not need something more?"

"It needs to be made better," said Annie, modestly.

"Yes, it needs to be placed in Jesus' hands to be made pure, and kept in the right way, here on earth, and then it will be his in the happy home in heaven. Does not Jesus hear when children pray, Annie?"

"I suppose so; but it seems as if he could not understand what children want, as he does grown-up people."

"Dear little Annie, you know that Jesus was once a child. You remember very well what happened yesterday. Jesus never forgets, he cannot forget. He remembers as well now when he was a little boy at Nazareth, as you do what you saw and heard but a moment ago. He knows what it is to live in a child's body, and to have a child's troubles. He had parents to obey, and young companions to make happy. He has not forgotten a child's feelings, he can sympathize with you, when no one else can. You must learn to love him, and to go to him in all your joys and troubles."

As Mr. Mayer closed, Annie looked up earnestly into his face, and said, with a great effort, three simple words—"I am trying." Three simple words they were, yet they filled the heart of the rector with pure joy. Poor little Annie! it cost her such a struggle to make this confession, that her eyes flowed out suddenly. It was, to her, a profession of Christ—her first owning to any human being that she wanted to take him for her Master. Mr. Mayer knelt down with the little girl, and spoke for her to the loving Saviour, who was once a child.

When Annie went forth from that room, it was with the pleasant thought that Jesus was to be with her by the way-side and in her home.

## CHAPTER XII.

### A BLACK SHADOW.

FARMER WATKINS'S eyes were heavy with sleep; he was for once weary— not with working, but with watching. He could have borne harvesting but with a single hand to help him, better than this standing by a sick-bed, day and night. A woman's business he said it was; and yet it was plain his heart was in it.

Farmer Watkins was a bachelor, and not much in the habit of looking out for other people's comfort; but there was one man on his place who had managed to get a hold upon him which seemed to triumph over selfishness. Farmer Watkins loved and respected Jack Tyler, and he could not see him stretched on a sick-bed without many a pang. Jack had been seized with a malignant fever; two days and nights his employer had been at his side, nursing him as tenderly as was consistent with his rough hands and rougher ways.

Now night was settling over the farm-house, and sleep seemed threatening to take an equally firm hold of the watcher. Farmer Watkins paced the room, shook himself, reminded himself of the medicines to be given at every half hour through the night. He looked at Jack, tossing, and murmuring strange nonsense, as the fever was on him. No! the good fellow should have proper care; with stern determination in his face, the farmer took his seat. His eyes, notwith-

standing his resolutions, were beginning to close, when there was a rap
at the outer door. A hand soon
beckoned the farmer from his post.

Mr. Mayer was in the hall below.
He had come, he said, to pass the
night with Jack. Farmer Watkins
looked at the minister, and exclaimed, "It's catchin', the fever is. You
are worth too much to be took down
that way. No, no! I can stand it
out a good piece longer."

The farmer felt very wide awake
in the fresh air of the hall, but when,
a half hour afterwards, he lay on his
own bed, he slept as if he was in
a trance, save that his deep snores
sounded through the house like the
voice of a trumpet.

Through the weary night hours
sat Mr. Mayer by the bed of Jack

12

Tyler. The sufferer knew a gentle hand ministered to him, and now and then a strange glance of half-puzzled recognition lighted up his features.

Those ravings, those muttered words of delirium, were poor companionship in the midnight hour; yet even in them the minister found comfort. They were but the upturning of a mind where evil had been allowed no resting-place, and habits of sin were strangers. Jack had fallen into a quiet doze, when, in the gray dawn, the farmer appeared at the door. Refreshed by his night's sleep, he realized all the more the kindness of the "friend in need" who had relieved him at his post, and his thanks were in proportion to his appreciation of the service rendered him.

A messenger on horseback had come with a summons for Mr. Mayer. The same fever that had prostrated the strong woodman, Jack Tyler, and closed for ever the eyes of old Katy Brown, has filled Augusta Berridge's veins with fire. Augusta's mind still had its power to think and reason; that power but rendered more fearful the agony she endured—agony both of body and mind. Her present sufferings seemed to bring before her a faint image of what might be in store for her soul—that soul to which she had given so little thought in her days of health. And was her mother her guide and comforter in this time of distress? Alas, for Mrs. Berridge! she knew not the Heavenly Friend after whom her daughter was feeling in the midst of a "horror of great darkness." She knew not the way to the foot of the cross; like Augusta, she was but beginning to seek that which she should first have sought, "the kingdom of heaven, and its righteousness."

Again and again, in Augusta's sick-room, Mr. Mayer had lifted up the voice of prayer. Where duty called, Marshall Mayer could go, though with every breath he might take in a fatal disease.

Now he urged his horse onward, as he hastened to the saddened home of Mrs. Berridge.

Annie noiselessly opened the door, and Charlie silently extended a hand to him in the hall. To the bedside of the altered girl he was promptly led.

Where was the sparkling vivacity

that had distinguished Augusta Berridge a few short weeks before? Sad, sunken eyes looked forth from her thin, pale face, and no words of sarcastic mirth came from her parched lips. Yet those lips had been able to cry, "God be merciful to me a sinner!"—those sad eyes had been lifted to Heaven.

Mr. Mayer knew that he was in the presence of a soul trembling on the brink of eternity; and O how tenderly, how faithfully he pictured the blessed Jesus, coming to seek and to save them that were lost. How, like a child drawing near to a father, he drew near to God, asking his best blessings of mercy for her who so "earnestly desired pardon and forgiveness."

Would the Saviour stoop to one

12*

sinner more, and lift her soul from the dust? Would Augusta Berridge be raised up to serve her Maker?

Who can tell the issues of life and death? Who knows, lying down at evening, if he will rise in the morning? Who knows when the petted body will sicken and die, and the neglected soul be called to account?

This only we know, "God waiteth to be gracious." Unto us he saith, "Now is the accepted time, now is the day of salvation."

# CHAPTER XIII.

## PURER AIR.

MEEDVILLE had been considered one of those healthy places, where it is of no use for young doctors to settle. There was no part of the quiet country town given up to wickedness and dirt, those great fosterers of disease and death.

Now and then an infant was laid in its quiet tomb, like a flower dropped on the bosom of mother earth. Now and then a hoary head drooped, as the ripened seed, and like that seed, was planted, to rise on the resurrection morn.

Occasionally some young, fair girl, or a man in the fulness of his strength, was called to lie down and die, as if to say, in words too startling to be mistaken, "Watch, therefore, for ye know not the day or the hour when the Son of Man cometh." So it had been at Meedville, since the now white-haired settlers made for themselves, in their youth, a home in the wilderness. No pestilence had ever prevailed in the favoured spot; and but for his own independent income, the slow-moving, cheerful-looking old doctor would have had to give up his profession, and devote himself to some more money-making business.

The sudden appearance of a malignant, contagious fever among them, had struck the people of Meedville with a fearful panic. The stout-hearted failed in this time of need;

and there were more to take the swift cars, and flee from the scene of contagion, than to stand by the bedsides of the sufferers, with the patient tenderness of a skilful nurse.

It was at this time that Marshall Mayer moved among the sick and dying, to soothe the pain-racked body, and comfort the sin-sick soul. He had no near relations to mourn his loss; no home would be left desolate if he were taken away. Perhaps these circumstances made it easier for him to peril his life where others dared not to go; but the great well-spring of his courage was his deep conviction that death could have no terrors for him, for *his* Lord had died.

The friends who gather round us in health, and add their joy to ours, are dear; but dearer are those who come to us when sickness makes dreary the family hearth, and silences the voice of mirth. Ah! how we prize the friend that comes like a sister to relieve the worn-out nurses, and give the sufferer a placid face to look upon, not yet marked with the weariness of long watching! How we welcome the manly form that can bow at the sick-bed with a woman's tenderness, yet lends its strength, like a rock, for the helpless to rest upon!

Years of ordinary ministry might have done less to draw Marshall Mayer near to his people than did those few dark, dark weeks, when fever hung round them like a plague. They could not but love the friend who had been their human stay in the time of their visitation, and had taught them where to seek for a support that would not fail them when called to go through the deep waters of affliction, or to enter the valley of the shadow of death. Mr. Mayer's regular, temperate life, and his vigorous constitution, had prepared him to endure great fatigue. Though Mrs. Toombs daily fretted at his exposing his valuable life, and daily looked to see him laid upon his sick-bed, he did but grow a little paler and thinner, while his face took a more and more sweetly placid expression. The good woman at length gave over her murmurings, and expended her energies in preparing cooling drinks for fevered lips, and nourishing food for the convalescents.

Health once more began to throb in Jack Tyler's veins. Augusta Berridge, too, was coming back to life, looking like a shadow from the spirit land. Jack was rising up to be doubly pledged to a life of usefulness, and Augusta thought her soul as much changed as her poor altered body. Her soul was changed truly; it was now her chief wish and purpose to obey and serve her Heavenly Father, rather than follow the evil promptings of her own evil nature. This change had taken place, but Augusta had her natural character to struggle with, her wrong habits to overcome. She had a work before her that could only be accomplished by watchfulness and prayer.

The cloud seemed to have passed away from Meedville, and many hearts were full of gratitude. White slabs had suddenly clustered among the moss-grown stones of the graveyard, and mourning garments had taken the place of gay attire; yet the scourge had proved a blessing, and "the Lord and Giver of life" had written many new names in his book of remembrance.

13

## CHAPTER XIV.

### A VESTRY-MEETING.

THE year for which Mr. Mayer had been engaged to supply the pulpit at Meedville had passed. Mrs. Toombs was restless and uneasy; but Charlie Clement was confident that his wishes were to be realized. The Vestry held their meeting; the very children in the street would have reproached them had their decision been other than it was.

Who should they have for their pastor? Who would so care for their souls, as the dear friend who had not hesitated to risk his life on their behalf? They knew who was welcome when the spirit saw eternity opening before it. They knew who could wipe away the mourner's tear, and whisper words of consolation. They knew who could win the hearts of their little ones, and lead them to Jesus. The meeting of the Vestry was but an occasion for expressing the rejoicing that Mr. Mayer could be retained among them. As with one voice they declared it their belief, that God had greatly blessed them in sending one to labour among them, who was such a faithful follower of his gracious Lord. Mr. Mayer's long years of loneliness had not deadened his heart to affection, and when his people, with a spontaneous movement, waited upon him to express their attachment, and to beg him to remain among them, his heart was so warmed and touched that his lips refused to speak, and but his moistened eyes, for a moment, gave answer; and then he broke forth in the touching words of Ruth—"This people shall be my people, and their God my God; and the Lord do so to me, and more also, if aught but death part them and me!"

And did the people of Meedville fancy they had secured perfection in their rector? No! They knew him to be "a man subject to like passions as themselves," heir of the same corruption, redeemed by the same Saviour, to be gradually sanctified by the same Spirit. Who but one struggling against sin could so feel for the tempted? Who better than a sinner clinging to the cross of Christ, could point out to the despairing the only sure refuge? Who but one "bought with a price," could devote himself body, soul, and spirit, to the work of his Heavenly Master?

Of our Saviour it is said, "Wherefore in all things it behooved him to be made like unto his brethren, that he might be a merciful and faithful high-priest, in things pertaining to God, to make reconciliation for the sins of the people. For in that he himself hath suffered being tempted, he is able to succour them that are tempted." If even the Lord Jesus took upon himself human flesh, that he might be our compassionate Redeemer, we need not wonder that no *perfect* men are sent among us as our ministers. God chooses in the midst of weakness to show his strength. To those who lean wholly upon him, in the fulfilment of their high com-

13*

mission, he gives a power to become holy, and a might to minister in his service, that redounds all the more to his honour for the weakness of the instrument employed. The people of Meedville had found no perfect being, but they had been blessed with the services of a true, conscientious, devoted Christian man. He was their ordained and instituted guide in the heavenly way. To him they meant to give not a pittance, but an abundant support; not criticism and opposition, but confidence and co-operation. They would join him in his prayers, hear him in his sermons, honour him by obedience to his counsel.

# CHAPTER XV.

### CONCLUSION.

CHARLIE CLEMENT was going home for his vacation. Home! His very heart leaped at the word. Dearer than ever seemed his mother to him, and he longed to be once more at her side. Mingled with all this joy was much regret at leaving Meedville, even for a short time. There were now many ties to bind him to his aunt's family circle, to his dear minister, and to the church, where he had first come forward to commemorate his Saviour's love.

Meedville would ever be dear to

him, a place around which the most delightful associations would cluster.

Charlie had been saying something like this to the family circle gathered about him on the morning of his departure.

"We shall all miss you sadly. I never had any idea before what a comfort a son might be to a widowed mother," said Mrs. Berridge, fondly.

"I can't bear to let you go," said Annie, drawing closer to her cousin, in her affectionate way. "I liked you at first, but lately you seem nicer—not so old, somehow."

"We must become as little children, if we would enter the kingdom of heaven," said Mr. Mayer, who was enjoying the last hour of Charlie's stay with him.

"Yes!" said Charlie, earnestly, and

his heart was full of humble joy. No parting gift could have been so precious to Charlie, as Annie's unconscious words. Had he then triumphed in a measure over his besetting sin! The thought was a spring to new exertion; new effort to seek the humility which is the crowning grace of the young Christian.

Mrs. Berridge was at this moment called out of the room. The visitor was no other than Mrs. Toombs, who modestly refused to enter the house farther than the dining-room. She no longer looked on Mrs. Berridge as her natural enemy, and had said, in her own queer way, "I was all wrong, to want nobody to sit by Mr. Mayer but me. The more friends he has, the better, I say now."

This morning she had come with

a basket of choice sandwiches for "Mr. Charlie to eat on the way, and to wish him good luck, as the warmest hearted boy that ever came to Meedville."

When Mrs. Berridge urged her to give her message in person, she shrunk back in dismay, and abruptly disappeared. Mrs. Toombs was still Mrs. Toombs, though profiting by the ministrations of her much-respected rector.

Mrs. Berridge returned to the parlour, and gave the basket and message to Charlie. Very welcome they both seemed.

"I like her, and I thank her," said Charlie. "We can't all be the same. Variety is the spice of life."

Augusta was going to hazard one of her old sharp remarks about Mrs.

Toombs. "But we don't want pepper in puddings, or Mrs. Toombs' peculiarities in a woman," she was going to say; but she changed her mind, and was silent. Augusta had learned something about the "unruly member," and was trying hard to govern it.

"Have you everything ready, Charlie?" said Mrs. Berridge, with a motherly, anxious look.

Charlie did not resent the imputation upon his skill as a traveller, but held up the cap in his hand, saying, "I have only this to put on, Aunt."

"And that you will have to do at once, for here is the hack at the door," said Augusta. "You have been a real good cousin to me, and I can't bear to spare you," she added, in a lower voice. "Your example has been a great deal to me!"

Annie had to let go her hold upon her cousin, and all the good-byes had to come to an end, for the cars would not wait, and the slow hack-horses must have full time allowed them.

"I am so glad I shall have you here when I come back," said Charlie to Mr. Mayer, when they were seated in the hack.

"And I am glad you are coming back," responded Mr. Mayer. "I have never told you, Charlie, how your bright young face broke in upon my studies, and changed the mere student into something like a pastor. Your visit was a real heart-warming to me. I shall miss you sadly."

"And what have you not done for

me?" said Charlie, earnestly, "poor, self-important boy that I was. If I ever am the humble Christian I want to be, I shall have to thank you for setting me on my guard against my besetting sin."

"Dear Charlie, every character has its own peculiar faults, to be struggled against with watchfulness and prayer. I will not speak of mine; but I must say that a loving, earnest, young parishioner, may do much for his minister, in his inner work, as well as his outward labours. God bless you, my boy, and sustain you in all your temptations until we meet again."

Very affectionate was the parting between Mr. Mayer and Charlie. Away went the happy lad to his mother and his home; back returned the minister to his well-beloved parish.

14

We need no prophet's eye to trace their future course. Each will go on as he has begun. Charlie will be the faithful, active, affectionate parishioner. Taking his heart in his right hand, and his purse in his left, he will devote his all to the service of his Maker, and ever be to his minister the tried and trusted friend; free to give his sympathy and his aid in every perplexity and every good work.

The Rev. Marshall Mayer will follow close upon the footsteps of his Divine Master. For the bodies as well as the souls of his people he will feel a tender interest. In their temporal trials, as in their spiritual need, he will be their comforter and their best adviser.

To him the hoary head will look up,

his hand will lead the children in the way. He will not sink under the responsibilities of his office. Cheerfully hopefully, he will go forward. Trusting in the Captain of his Salvation, he will be sure to come off victorious. For him will be "laid up a crown of rejoicing," when he shall appear in the kingdom of the redeemed. For him will sound the voice of welcome at the gates of the heavenly city.

THE END.

# ATTRACTIVE JUVENILE BOOKS

## PUBLISHED BY

## WILLIAM S. & ALFRED MARTIEN,

### 606 Chestnut Street, Philadelphia.

---

### DICK AND HIS FRIEND FIDUS.

By C. M. Trowbridge. Illustrated. 18mo. 45 cts.

This is a capital story for boys; we have not read a better one for some time. Dick always comes out right and safe when he obeys Fidus, but has a sad experience at other times.—*Congregational Herald.*

### CHARLES NORWOOD;

Or, Erring and Repenting. By C. M. Trowbridge. Illustrated. 16mo. 75 cents.

The story of the trials, temptations, and sufferings of a young New York merchant, with the picture of as lovely a family as the imagination could paint.

### PLAIN WORDS TO YOUNG MEN.

By Rev. J. B. Ripley. 18mo. 25 cents.

A powerfully written series of exhortations to avoid the snares and temptations which peculiarly beset young men, and well illustrated by anecdotes. No one can read this little book without feeling that it is written in earnest, and not merely for the sake of obtaining a name. It is divided into five parts, viz., the young man adrift; the young man anchored; the young man at home; the young man in the world; and the young man at the end.

### BUY AN ORANGE, SIR?

Or, the History of Jamie Woodford. Illustrated. 18mo. 25 cents.

A delightful story, well told, and full of instruction.

1

## MELODIES FOR CHILDHOOD.

With Thirty fine Illustrations. 16mo. 75 cts.

The richest collection of Melodies for Children we have ever seen.

## DIDLEY DUMPS;

Or, the Story of John Ellard, the Newsboy. Illustrated. 18mo. 50 cents.

We should love to scatter this little book by the thousand. We regard it as a model of simplicity. He who can read it without tears of sympathy for the outcast and neglected, and without prayers that they may be saved, hath a hard nature. It is the story of a poor little hump-backed newsboy, who by kindness and love was won from the paths of sin to the feet of a forgiving and loving Saviour. He died in his bed, after having been frequently helped by newsboys' hands into an attitude of prayer. The book is both an argument for missionary work among the poor and the neglected, and a beautiful illustration of what that work may accomplish.—*Christian Chronicle.*

## NO LIE THRIVES.

A book for Boys. By the author of "Charlie Burton." Illustrated. 18mo. 50 cents.

A tale of deep interest, well conceived, and skilfully constructed. It forcibly portrays the evils of deceit and falsehood, and, on the contrary, the advantages of a strict adherence to truth.—*Presbyterian.*

## MARK NOBLE;

Or, the Button Necklace. Illustrated. 18mo. 30 cents.

This is a story of two deserted orphan children, who were left to the sorrows and the temptations of the streets of London.—*Christian Chronicle.*

2

## WILLIE AND NELLIE;

Or, Stories about My Canaries. **By Cousin Sarah.** Square 16mo. Illustrated. 50 cents

This little book is full of pleasantly told stories about these pet birds, and is exactly calculated to please and interest little children.—*Epis. Recorder.*

## MAMMA'S LESSONS ABOUT JESUS.

By a Mother. With four beautiful Illustrations. 12mo. 75 cents.

We cordially commend this book to mothers who are desirous of imbuing the tender minds of their children with the saving truths of the evangelical history. It is simple without being childish, or in any way lowering the dignity of the sacred narrative. We have seldom met with a book of the kind which has pleased us so well. Let mothers try it in the instruction of their children.

## BLIND TOM;

Or, the Lost Found. With four Illustrations. 18mo. 50 cents.

The authoress has succeeded in throwing around the history of a friendless little boy an unusual charm by her natural and happy method of portraying the incidents of his life. Some of the scenes are graphic and touching, evincing no ordinary ability in the writer as a delineator of character.

## ROBERT AND HAROLD;

Or, the Young Marooners on the Florida Coast. By F. R. Goulding. With Twelve Illustrations. Eighth thousand. 16mo. 75 cents.

There is in this little volume for the young, a singular blending of fact with fiction, of curious and useful information with exciting adventure; such as almost tempts us to set it apart as a new species of juvenile literature. The adventures of the Young Marooners are nearly as wild and exciting as Robinson Crusoe; and yet we understand the author to say they are substantially true. The incidents of the

3

story are adroitly arranged to bring into view a great variety of curious information, much of which is as useful as it is novel and stirring. Altogether we do not hesitate to say that it is a remarkable little book; and will undoubtedly become a great favourite with the young, as it well deserves the confidence and favour of parents.—*Biblical Repertory*.

## HEIGHTS OF EIDELBERG;

By Helen Hazlett. Illustrated. 16mo. 75 cents.

A story of absorbing interest.

## IDOLETTE STANLEY;

Or, The Beauty of Discipline. Illustrated. 16mo. 75 cents.

The story of a petted child, and her trials in conquering herself into submission to the better sense and discretion of her elders.

## INFLUENCE.

A Moral Tale for Young People. By Charlotte Anley, author of "Miriam." 16mo. 75 cents.

A delightful story, full of pure sentiment and elevated moral.—*Inquirer*.

*By the Author of the Basket of Flowers.*

### I.
## THE BASKET OF FLOWERS;

Or, Piety and Truth Triumphant. With Illustrations. Sixteenth edition. 18mo. 31 cents.

### II.
## ROSA, OF LINDEN CASTLE;

Or, Filial Affection. A Tale for Parents and Children. Illustrated. 18mo. 50 cents.

### III.
## THE RINGS;

Or, the Two Orphans. Illustrated. 18mo. 31 cents.

4